THE STORY OF Little Christmas

by
— GEORGE MACDONALD —
Illustrated by Tom Gianni

Chariot Books™
*A Division of Cook
Communications Ministries*

*The pictures in this book are dedicated to my parents,
Louis and Margaret, with gratitude and everlasting love.*
T.G.

ACKNOWLEDGEMENTS:
Special thanks to the Marion E. Wade Collection, Wheaton College, Wheaton, Illinois, for the use of materials from the George MacDonald collection, and for the staff's assistance in obtaining these materials.

"The Story of Little Christmas" was originally titled "My Uncle Peter" and is abridged and adapted from ADELA CATHCART, Loring Publisher, Boston, ca. 1870.

"My Uncle Peter" is also published in *The Christmas Stories of George MacDonald*, David C. Cook Publishing, 1981.

Chariot Books™ is an imprint of Chariot Family Publishing
Cook Communications Ministries, Elgin, Illinois 60120
Cook Communications Ministries, Paris, Ontario
Kingsway Communications, Eastbourne, England

THE STORY OF LITTLE CHRISTMAS

Cover design by Jack Rogers
Cover illustration by Tom Gianni
First printing, 1995
Printed in The United States of America
99 98 97 96 95 5 4 3 2 1

I will tell you the story of Little Christmas and my Uncle Peter, who both were born on Christmas Day. Uncle was very anxious to die on Christmas Day as well. But I must confess that was rather ambitious of him. Shakespeare is said to have been born on St. George's Day, and there is some ground for believing that he died on St. George's Day. He thus fulfilled a cycle. But we cannot expect that of any but great men. And Uncle Peter was not a great man, though I think I shall be able to show that he was a good man.

Uncle Peter was a little, round man, not very fat, resembling both in limbs and features an overgrown baby. And I believe the resemblance was not merely an external one. For, though his intellect was quite up to par, he retained a degree of simplicity of character and of tastes that bordered, sometimes, upon the childish.

"Ah, my dear," he would say to my mother when she scolded him for making some present far beyond the small means he at that time possessed, "ah, my dear, you see I was born on Christmas Day."

He lived upstairs in our house, and was pretty sure to be found seated in his easy chair, for he was fond of his simple comforts, beside a good fire, reading by the light of one candle. He had his tea always as soon as he came home, and some buttered toast or a hot muffin, of which he was sure to make me eat three-quarters, which, I am rather ashamed to say, I not unfrequently did.

One Christmas Eve we had been occupied, as usual, with the presents of the following Christmas Day. I was helping him to make up parcels, when from a sudden impulse, I said to him, "How good you are, my uncle!"

"Ha! ha! ha!" laughed he. "That's the best joke of all. Good, my boy! Ha! ha! ha!"

Then my uncle's face grew suddenly very grave, even sad in its expression. After a pause he resumed, but this time without any laughing. "Good, Charlie! Why, I'm no use to anybody."

"You do me good, anyhow, Uncle," I answered.

"I wish I could be of real, unmistakable use to any one," he continued. "But I fear I am not good enough to have that honor done me."

ext morning—Christmas Day—we went out for a walk. Uncle Peter's usual generosity had increased since coming into a rather large inheritance, and he often gave freely to people in need. Nothing less than a three-penny piece would do for a crossing sweeper on Christmas Day; but one tiny little girl touched his heart so that the usual coin was doubled. Still this did not relieve the heart of the giver sufficiently; for the child looked up in his face in a way, whatever the way was, that made his heart ache. So he gave her a shilling. But he felt no better after that.

This won't do, said Uncle Peter to himself. "What is your name?"

"Little Christmas," she answered.

"Little Christmas!" exclaimed Uncle Peter. "I see why that wouldn't do now. What do you mean?"

"Little Christmas, sir."

"What's your father's name?"

"I ain't got none, sir."

"But you know what his name was?"

"No, sir."

"How did you get your name then? It must be the same as your father's, you know."

"Then I suppose my father was Christmas Day, sir, for I knows of none else. They always calls me Little Christmas."

H'm! A little sister of mine, I see, said Uncle Peter to himself. "Well, who's your mother?"

"My aunt, sir. She knows I'm out, sir."

There was not the least impudence in the child's tone or manner in saying this. She looked up at him with her dark eyes in the most confident manner.

"Is your aunt kind to you?"

"She gives me my supper."

"Suppose you did not get any money all day, what would she say to you?"

"Oh, she won't give me a hidin' today, sir, supposin' I gets no more. You've giv' me enough already, sir. Thank you, sir. I'll change it into ha'pence."

"She does beat you sometimes, then?"

"Oh, my!"

Here she rubbed her arms and elbows as if she ached all over at the thought, and these were the only parts she could reach to rub for the whole.

*will,* said Uncle Peter to himself. "Do you think you were born on Christmas Day, little one?"

"I think I was once, sir."

"Will you go home with us?" he said, coaxingly.

"Yes, sir, if you will tell me where to put my broom, for I must not go home without it, else Aunt would wallop me."

"I will buy you a new broom."

"But Aunt would wallop me all the same if I did not bring home the old one for our Christmas fire."

"Never mind. I will take care of you. You may bring your broom if you like, though," he added, seeing a cloud come over the little face.

"Thank you, sir," said the child. Shouldering her broom, she trotted along behind him, as he led the way home.

But this would not do, either. Before they had gone twelve paces, Uncle Peter had the child in one hand; and before they had gone a second twelve, he had the broom in the other. And so Uncle Peter walked home with Little Christmas and her broom. The latter he set down inside the door, and the former he led upstairs to the sitting room. There he seated her on a chair by the fire, and asked my mother to bring a basin of bread and milk.

The child sat with her feet wide apart, and reaching halfway down the legs of the chair, and her black eyes staring from the midst of knotted tangles of hair that never felt comb or brush, or were defended from the wind by bonnet or hood. I dare say the room, with its cases of stuffed birds and its square piano that was used for a cupboard, seemed to her the most sumptuous of conceivable abodes. But she said nothing—only stared. When her bread and milk came, she ate it up without a word, and when she had finished it sat still for a moment, as if pondering what it became her to do next. Then she rose, dropped a curtsy, and said, "Thank you, sir. Please, sir, where's my broom?"

"Oh, but I want you to stay with us, and be our little girl."

"Please, sir, I would rather go to my crossing." The face of Little Christmas lengthened visibly, and she was upon the point of crying. Uncle Peter saw that he must woo the child before he could hope to win her. The best way seemed to promise her a new frock on the morrow, if she would come and fetch it. Her face brightened at the sound of a new frock.

"Will you know the way back, my dear?"

"I always know my way anywheres," answered she. So she was allowed to depart with her cherished broom.

ncle Peter took my mother into council upon the affair of the frock. She thought an old one of my sister's would do best. But my uncle had said a *new* frock, and a new one it must be. So next day my mother went with him to buy one, and was excessively amused with his entire ignorance of what was suitable for the child. However, once the frock was purchased, he saw how absurd it would be to put a new frock over such garments as she must have below, and accordingly made my mother buy everything to clothe her completely.

With these treasures he hastened home, and found poor Little Christmas and her broom waiting for him outside the door. My mother washed her with her own soft hands from head to foot, and then put all the new clothes on her. She looked charming. My uncle was delighted at the improvement in her appearance. I saw him turn round and wipe his eyes with his handkerchief.

"Now, Little Christmas, will you come and live with us?" said he.

She pulled the same face, though not quite so long as before, and said, "I would rather go to my crossing, please, sir."

My uncle heaved a sigh and let her go.

Little Christmas shouldered her broom, as if it had been the rifle of a giant, and trotted away to her work.

But next day, and the next, and the next, she was not to be seen at her wonted corner. When a whole week had passed and she did not make her appearance, my family became worried, and my uncle was in despair.

"You see, Charlie," said he, "I am fated to be of no use to anybody, though I was born on Christmas Day."

The very next day, however, being Sunday, my uncle found her as we went to church. She was sweeping a new crossing. All her new clothes were gone, and she was more tattered and wretched-looking than before. As soon as she saw my uncle, she burst into tears.

"Look," she said, pulling up her little frock and showing her thigh with a terrible bruise upon it. "*She* did it."

A fresh burst of tears followed.

"Where are your new clothes, Little Christmas?" asked my uncle.

"She sold them for gin, and then beat me awful. Please, sir, I couldn't help it."

The child's tears were so bitter, that my uncle, without thinking, said, "Never mind, dear; you shall have another frock."

Her tears ceased, and her face brightened for a moment. But the weeping returned almost instantaneously with increased violence, and she sobbed out, "It's no use, sir; she'd only serve me the same, sir."

"Will you come home and live with us, then?"

"Yes, please."

She flung her broom from her into the middle of the street, nearly throwing down a cab horse, betwixt whose forelegs it tried to pass. Then she put her hand in that of her friend and trotted home with him.

9

nce more the little stray lamb was washed and clothed from head to foot, and from skin to frock.

My uncle never allowed her to go out without one of the family, or someone who was capable of protecting her. He did not think it at all necessary to supply the woman, who might not be her aunt after all, with gin unlimited, for the privilege of rescuing Little Christmas from her cruelty. So he felt that she was in great danger of being carried off, for the sake either of her earnings or her ransom. In fact, some very suspicious-looking characters were several times observed prowling about in the neighborhood.

Chrissy, as we came to call her, was a sweet-tempered, loving child. But the love seemed for some time to have no way of showing itself, so little had she been used to ways of love and tenderness. When we kissed her, she never returned the kiss, but only stared; and ugly words would now and then break from her dear, little, innocent lips. Yet whatever we asked her to do she would do as if her whole heart was in it, and I did not doubt it was.

After a few years, when Chrissy began to be considered tolerably capable of taking care of herself, the vigilance of my uncle gradually relaxed a little. A month before her thirteenth birthday, as near as my uncle could guess, the girl disappeared. She had gone to the day school as usual, and was expected home in the afternoon. But she did not return at the usual hour.

y uncle went to inquire about her. She had left the school with the rest. Night drew on. My family was in despair. Uncle roamed the streets all night, spoke about Chrissy to every policeman he met, went to the station house of the district and described her. He had bills printed, and offered a hundred pounds reward for her restoration. All was unavailing.

Before the month was out, his clothes were hanging about him like a sack. He could hardly swallow a mouthful, hardly even sit down to a meal. I believe he loved his Little Christmas every whit as much as if she had been his own daughter—perhaps more—for he could not help thinking of what she might have been if he had not rescued her. He felt that God had given her to us as certainly as if she had been his own child. He would get out of bed in the middle of the night, unable to sleep, and go wandering up and down the streets, and into dreadful places, sometimes, to try to find her.

But fasting and watching could not go on long without bringing worse things with them. Uncle Peter was seized with a fever, which grew and grew till his life was despaired of. He was very delirious at times, and then the strangest fancies had possession of his brain. Sometimes he seemed to see the horrid woman she called her aunt, torturing the poor child. The doctors seemed doubtful, and gave as their opinions a decided shake of the head.

Two days before Christmas, Uncle was still deeply saddened. In the afternoon, to the wonder of all about him, although he had been wandering a moment before, he suddenly said, "I was born on Christmas Day, you know. This will be the first Christmas Day that didn't bring me good luck."

Turning to me, he added, "Charlie, my boy, it's a good thing *Another* besides me was born on Christmas Day, isn't it?"

"Yes, dear uncle," said I. It was all I could say. He lay quite quiet for a few minutes, when there came a gentle knock to the street door.

T hat's Chrissy!" he cried, starting up in bed, and stretching out his arms with trembling eagerness. "And I said this Christmas Day would bring me no good!"

He fell back on his pillow, and burst into a flood of tears.

I rushed down to the door and reached it before the servant. I stared. There stood a girl about the size of Chrissy, with an old, battered bonnet on, and a ragged shawl. She was standing on the doorstep, trembling. She had Chrissy's eyes, too, I thought. But the light was dim now, for the evening was coming on.

"What is it?" I said, in a tremor of expectation.

"Charlie, don't you know me?" she said, and burst into tears.

"Chrissy!" I said, and we were in each other's arms in a moment. I led her upstairs in triumph, and into my uncle's room.

"I knew it was my lamb!" he cried, stretching out his arms, and trying to lift himself up, only he was too weak.

Chrissy flew to his arms and embraced him as she never had before. She was very dirty, and her clothes had such a smell of poverty! But there she lay in my uncle's bosom, both of them sobbing, for a long time. When at last she withdrew, she tumbled down on the floor, and there she lay motionless. I was in a dreadful fright, but my mother came in at the moment and got her into a warm bath, and lovingly put her to bed.

In the morning she was much better, and when she entered the room dressed in her own nice clothes, my uncle stretched out his arms to her once more and said, "Ah! Chrissy, I thought I was going to have my own way, and die on Christmas Day; but it would have been one too soon, before I had found you, my darling."

It was resolved that, on that same day, Chrissy should tell us her story.

After my uncle's afternoon nap was over, Chrissy got up on the bed beside him. I got up at the foot of the bed, facing her, and we had the tea tray and plenty of *etceteras* between us. My mother and sister sat nearby.

"Oh! I *am* happy!" said Chrissy, and began to cry.

"So am I, my darling!" rejoined Uncle Peter, and followed her example.

"So am I," said I, "but I don't mean to cry about it." And then I did.

We all had one cup of tea, and some bread and butter in silence after this. But when Chrissy had poured out the second cup for Uncle Peter, she began to tell us her story.

t was very foggy when we came out of school that afternoon, as you may remember, dear uncle."

"Indeed I do," answered Uncle Peter, with a sigh.

"I was coming along the way home with Bessie—you know Bessie, Uncle—and we stopped to look in at the bookseller's window, where the gas was lighted. It was full of Christmas things already. One of them I thought very pretty, and I was standing staring at it, when all at once I saw that a big, drabby woman had poked herself in between Bessie and me. She was staring in at the window too. She was so nasty that I moved away a little from her, but I wanted to have one more look at the picture. The woman came close to me. I moved again. Again she pushed up to me. I looked in her face, for I was rather cross by this time.

"A horrid feeling came over me as soon as I saw her. I did not know then why I was frightened. I think she saw I was frightened, for she instantly walked against me, and shoved and hustled me round the corner. Before I knew, I was in another street. It was dark and narrow. Just at that moment a man came from the opposite side and joined the woman. Then they caught hold of my hands, and before my fright would let me speak I was deep into the narrow lane, for they ran with me as fast as they could.

"I began to scream, but they said such horrid words that I was forced to hold my tongue. In a minute more they had me inside a dreadful house, where the plaster was dropping away from the walls and the skeleton ribs of the house were looking through. I was nearly dead with terror and disgust. I don't think it was a bit less dreadful to me from having dim recollection of having known such places well enough at one time of my life. I think that only made me the more frightened, because the place seemed to have a claim upon me. What if I ought to be there, after all, and these dreadful creatures were my father and mother!

I thought they were going to beat me at once, when the woman, whom I suspected to be my aunt, began to take off my frock. I was dreadful frightened, but I could not cry. However, it was only my clothes that they wanted. But I cannot tell you how frightful it was. They took almost everything I had on, and it was only when I began to scream in despair that they stopped, with a nod to each other, as much as to say, *We can get the rest afterwards.* Then they put a filthy frock on me, brought me some dry bread to eat, locked the door, and left me. It was nearly dark now. There was no fire. All my warm clothes were gone, and I was dreadfully cold. There was a wretched-looking bed in one corner; but I think I would have died of cold rather than get into it. And the air in the place was frightful. How long I sat there in the dark, I don't know."

"What did you do all the time?" said I.

"There was only one thing to be done, Charlie. I think that is a foolish question to ask."

"Well, what *did* you do, Chrissy?"

"Said my prayers, Charlie," Chrissy answered.

"And then?"

"Said them again. Then I tried to get out of the window, but that was of no use; for I could not open it. And it was one story high at least."

"And what did you do next?"

"Well, I will tell you. I left my prayers alone, and I began at the beginning. I told God the whole story, as if he had known nothing about it, from when Uncle Peter found me on the crossing down to the minute when I was talking there to him in the dark.

By and by I heard a noise of quarreling in the street, which came nearer and nearer. The door was burst open by someone falling against it. Blundering steps came upstairs. The two who had robbed me, evidently tipsy, were trying to unlock the door. At length they succeeded, and tumbled into the room.

" 'Where is the unnatural wretch?' said the woman.

"Well, she began groping about to find me, for it was very dark. I sat quite still, except for trembling all over, till I felt her hands on me. When I jumped up, she fell on the floor. She began swearing dreadfully, but did not try to get up. I crept away to another corner. I heard the man snoring, and the woman breathing loud. Then I felt my way to the door, but, to my horror, found the man lying across it on the floor so that I could not open it. Then I believe I cried for the first time. I was nearly frozen to death, and there was all the long night to bear yet.

"How I got through it, I cannot tell. It did go away. Perhaps God destroyed some of it for me. But when the light began to come through the window, and show me all the filth of the place, the man and the woman lying on the floor, the woman with her head cut and covered with blood, I began to feel that the darkness had been my friend. I felt this yet more when I saw the state of my own dress, which I had forgotten in the dark. It was an old gown of some woolen stuff, but it was impossible to tell what. I was ashamed that even those drunken creatures should wake and see me in it.

"But the light *would* come, and it came and came, until at last it waked them up, and the first words were so dreadful! They quarreled and swore at each other and at me until I almost thought there couldn't be a God who would let that go on so, and never stop it. But I suppose He wants them to stop, and doesn't care to stop it Himself, for He could easily do that of course, if He liked."

"Just right, my darling!" said Uncle Peter, with emotion.

Chrissy saw that my uncle, still in poor health, was too much excited by her story, although he tried not to show it, and with wisdom she cut it short.

"They did not treat me cruelly, though. The worst was, that they gave me next to nothing to eat. Perhaps they wanted to make me thin and wretched-looking, and I believe they succeeded.

"Three days passed this way. I have thought all over it, and I think they were a little puzzled how to get rid of me. They had no doubt watched me for a long time, and now that they had got my clothes, they were afraid.

"At last one night they took me out. My aunt, if aunt she is, was respectably dressed—that is, comparatively—and the man had a greatcoat on, which covered his dirty clothes. They helped me into a cart, which stood at the door, and drove off. I resolved to watch the way we went. But we took so many turnings through narrow streets before we came out in a main road, that I soon found it was all one mass of confusion in my head; and it was too dark to read any of the names of the streets, for the man kept as much in the middle of the road as possible.

He drove some miles, I should think, before we stopped at the gate of a small house with a big porch, which stood alone. My aunt got out and went up to the house, and was admitted. After a few minutes she returned, and, making me get out, she led me up to the house, where an elderly lady stood, holding the door half open. When we reached it, my aunt gave me a sort of shove in, saying to the lady, 'There she is.' Then she said to me, 'Come now, be a good girl, and don't tell lies,' and, turning hastily, ran down the steps, and got into the cart at the gate, which drove off at once the way we had come.

"The lady looked at me from head to foot, sternly but kindly, too, I thought, and so glad was I to find myself clear of those dreadful creatures, that I burst out crying. She instantly began to read me a lecture on the privilege of being placed with good people, who would teach me to lead an honest and virtuous life. I tried to say that I had led an honest life. But as often as I opened my mouth to tell anything about myself or my uncle, or, indeed, to say anything at all, I was stopped by her saying, 'Now don't tell lies. Whatever you do, don't tell lies.' This shut me up quite. I could not speak when I knew she would not believe me.

"You may be sure I made haste to put on the nice clean frock she gave me, and, to my delight, found other clean things for me as well. I declare I felt like a princess for a whole day after, notwithstanding the occupation. For I soon found that I had been made over to Mrs. Sprinx, as a servant of all work. I think she must have paid these people for the chance of reclaiming one whom they had represented as at least a great liar. Whether my wages were to be paid to them, or even what they were to be, I never heard. I made up my mind at once that the best thing would be to do the work without grumbling, and do it as well as I could, for that would be doing no harm to any one and give me a better chance of escape.

22

ut though I was determined to get away at the first opportunity, and was miserable when I thought how anxious you would all be about me, yet I confess it was such a relief to be clean and in respectable company, that I caught myself singing once or twice the very first day. But the old lady soon stopped that. She was about in the kitchen the greater part of the day till dinner time, and taught me how to cook and save my soul both at once.

"I had finished washing up my dinner things, and sat down for a few minutes, for I was tired. I was staring into the fire, and thinking and thinking how I should get back to Uncle Peter and all of you, when suddenly I saw a little boy in a corner of the kitchen, staring at me with great brown eyes. I did not speak to him, but waited to see what he would do. A few minutes passed, and I forgot him. But as I was wiping my eyes, which would get wet sometimes, he came up to me, and said in a timid whisper, 'Are you a princess?'

" 'What makes you think that?' I said.

" 'You have got such white hands,' he answered.

" 'No, I am not a princess.'

" 'Aren't you Cinderella?'

" 'No, my darling,' I replied.

'But something like her; for they have stolen me away from home and brought me here. I wish I could get away.'

"And here I confess I burst into a downright fit of crying.

" 'Don't cry,' said the little fellow, stroking my cheek. 'I will let you out sometime. Shall you be able to find your way home all by yourself?'

" 'Yes, I think so,' I answered. But at the same time I felt very doubtful about it, because I always fancied those people watching me. But before either of us spoke again, in came Mrs. Sprinx.

" 'You naughty boy! What business have you to make the servant neglect her work?'

"For I was still sitting by the fire, and my arm was round the dear little fellow, and his head was leaning on my shoulder.

" 'She's not a servant, Auntie!' cried he, indignantly. 'She's a real princess, though of course she won't own to it.'

" 'What lies you have been telling the boy! You ought to be ashamed of yourself. Come along directly. Get the tea at once, Jane.'

y little friend went with his aunt, and I rose and got the tea. But I felt much lighter hearted since I had the sympathy of the little boy to comfort me. Only I was afraid they would make him hate me. But, although I saw very little of him the rest of the time, I knew they had not succeeded in doing so. As often as he could, he would come sliding up to me, saying, 'How do you do, Princess?' and then run away, afraid of being seen and scolded.

"I was getting very desperate about making my escape, for there was a high wall about the place, and the gate was always locked at night. When I saw Christmas Eve was coming, I was nearly crazy with thinking that it would soon be Uncle's birthday and I should not be with him. But one night, after I had gone to my room, the door opened, and in came little Eddie in his nightgown, his eyes looking very bright and black over it.

" 'There, Princess!' said he. 'There is the key of the gate. Run.'

"I took him in my arms and kissed him, unable to speak. He struggled to get free, and ran to the door. There he turned and said, 'You will come back and see me some day. Will you not?'

" 'That I will,' I answered."

"That you shall," said Uncle Peter.

I hid the key, and went to bed, where I lay trembling. As soon as I was sure they must be asleep, I rose and dressed. I had no bonnet or shawl but those I had come in. Though they disgusted me, I thought it better to put them on. But I dared not unlock the street door, for fear of making a noise. So I crept out of the kitchen window, and then I got out at the gate all safe. No one was in sight. So I locked it again, and threw the key over.

"But what a time of fear and wandering about I had in the darkness before I dared to ask anyone the way! It was a bright, clear night, and I walked very quietly till I came upon a great wide common. The sky and the stars and the wideness frightened me, and made me gasp at first. I felt as if I should fall away from everything into nothing. But then I thought of God, and grew brave again, and walked on. When the morning dawned, I met a bricklayer going to his work, and found that I had been wandering away from London all the time. But I did not mind that. Now I turned my face towards it, though not the way I had come. I soon got dreadfully tired and faint, and once I think I fainted quite. I went up to a house, and asked for a piece of bread, and they gave it to me, and I felt much better after eating it. But I had to rest so often, and got so tired, and my feet got so sore, that— you know how late it was before I got home."

"This shan't happen any more!" said my uncle.

After tea was over, he wrote a note, which he sent off.

On Christmas morning, about eleven, as I was looking out of the window, I saw a carriage drive up and stop at our door.

"What a pretty little carriage!" I cried. "And such a jolly horse! Look here, Chrissy!"

Miss Chrissy was sent for. She came down, radiant with pleasure.

"What do you think, Charlie! That carriage is mine—all my own. And I am to go to school in it always. Do come and have a ride in it."

"Where shall we go?" I said.

"Let us ask Uncle if we may go and see the little darling who set me free."

His consent was soon obtained, and away we went. It was a long drive, but we enjoyed it beyond everything. When we reached the house, we were shown into the drawing room. There was Mrs. Sprinx and little Eddie. The lady stared; but the child knew Cinderella at once, and flew into her arms.

"I knew you were a princess!" he cried. "There, Auntie!"

But Mrs. Sprinx had put on an injured look and her hands shook very much. "Really, Miss Belper, if that is your name, you have behaved in a most unaccountable way. Why did you not tell me, instead of stealing the key of the gate and breaking the kitchen window? A most improper way for a young lady to behave—to run out of the house at midnight!"

"You forget, madam," replied Chrissy, revealing her ill temper for the first time, "that as soon as I attempted to open my mouth, you told me not to tell lies. You believed the wicked people who brought me here rather than myself. However, as you will not be friendly, I think we had better go. Come, Charlie!"

"Don't go, Princess," pleaded little Eddie.

"But I must, for your auntie does not like me," said Chrissy haughtily.

"I am sure I always meant to do the best for you. And I will do so still. Beware, my dear young woman, of the deceitfulness of riches. Your money won't save your soul!" Mrs. Sprinx said.

Chrissy was on the point of saying something else rude, but she simply turned and walked away. I followed.

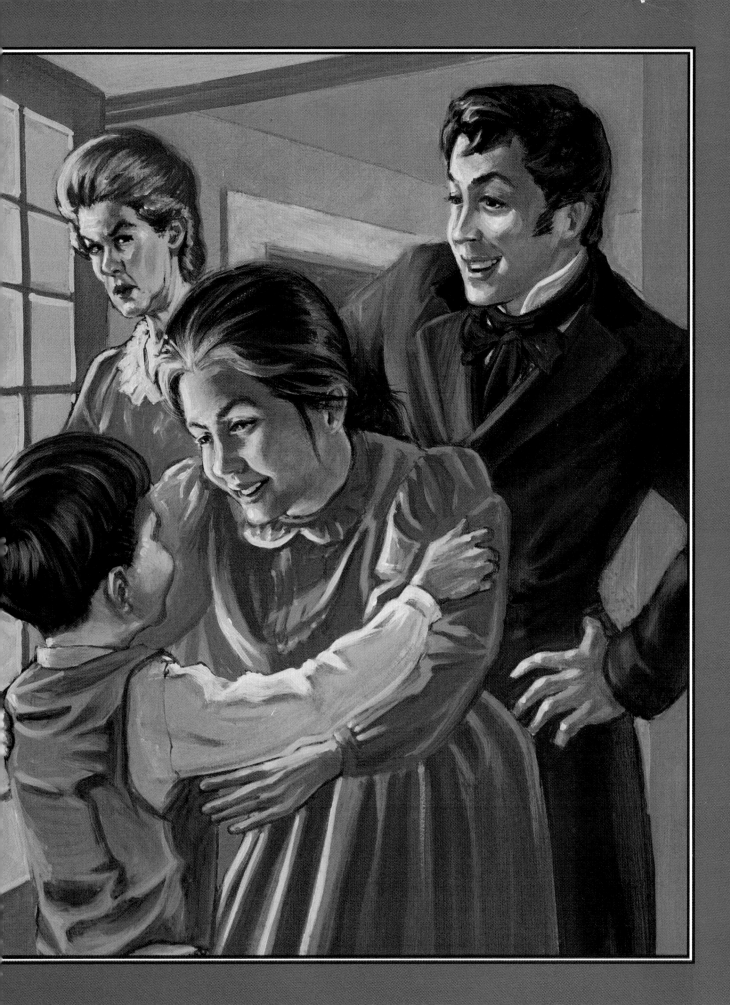

I confess this was not quite proper behavior on Chrissy's part. She was very sorry afterwards. While she had accepted our family's love, she had only just begun to understand how to forgive. When she narrated the whole story to my uncle, his look first let her see that she had been wrong.

Uncle Peter went with her afterwards to see Mrs. Sprinx and thank her for having done her best, and to take Eddie such presents as my uncle only knew how to buy for children.

From that time till now, Chrissy has had no more such adventures. And if Uncle Peter did not die on Christmas Day, it did not matter much, for Christmas Day makes all the days of the year as sacred as itself.